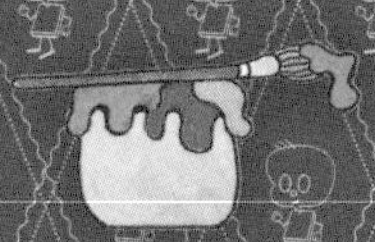

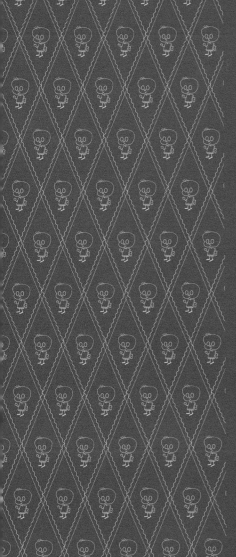

CHICK & CHICKIE

PLAY ALL DAY!

Claude Ponti

CHICK & CHICKIE

PLAY ALL DAY!

AAAH!

A TOON BOOK BY

Claude Ponti

TOON BOOKS IS AN IMPRINT OF CANDLEWICK PRESS

For Adèle

Editorial Director: FRANÇOISE MOULY

Book Design: JONATHAN BENNETT & FRANÇOISE MOULY

CLAUDE PONTI'S artwork was done in ink and watercolors.

 Printed in Singapore by Tien Wah Press (Pte.) Ltd. Library of Congress Cataloging-in-Publication Data:

Ponti, Claude, 1948-

Chick & Chickie play all day! / by Claude Ponti.

p. cm. "A TOON book." Based on two of the author's books, previously published in French: Tromboline et Foulbazar : les masques, and Tromboline et Foulbazar : le A.

Summary: Two young chicks have fun making masks and playing with the letter A.

ISBN 978-1-935179-14-6 (hardcover : alk. paper)

1. Graphic novels. [1. Graphic novels. 2. Chickens–Fiction. 3. Play–Fiction.] I. Title. II. Title. Chick and Chickie play all day!

PZ7.7.P66Ch 2012 741.5'944–dc23 2011026764

ISBN 13: 978-1-935179-14-6 ISBN 10: 1-935179-14-4

12 13 14 15 16 17 TWP 10 9 8 7 6 5 4 3 2 1

www.TOON-BOOKS.com

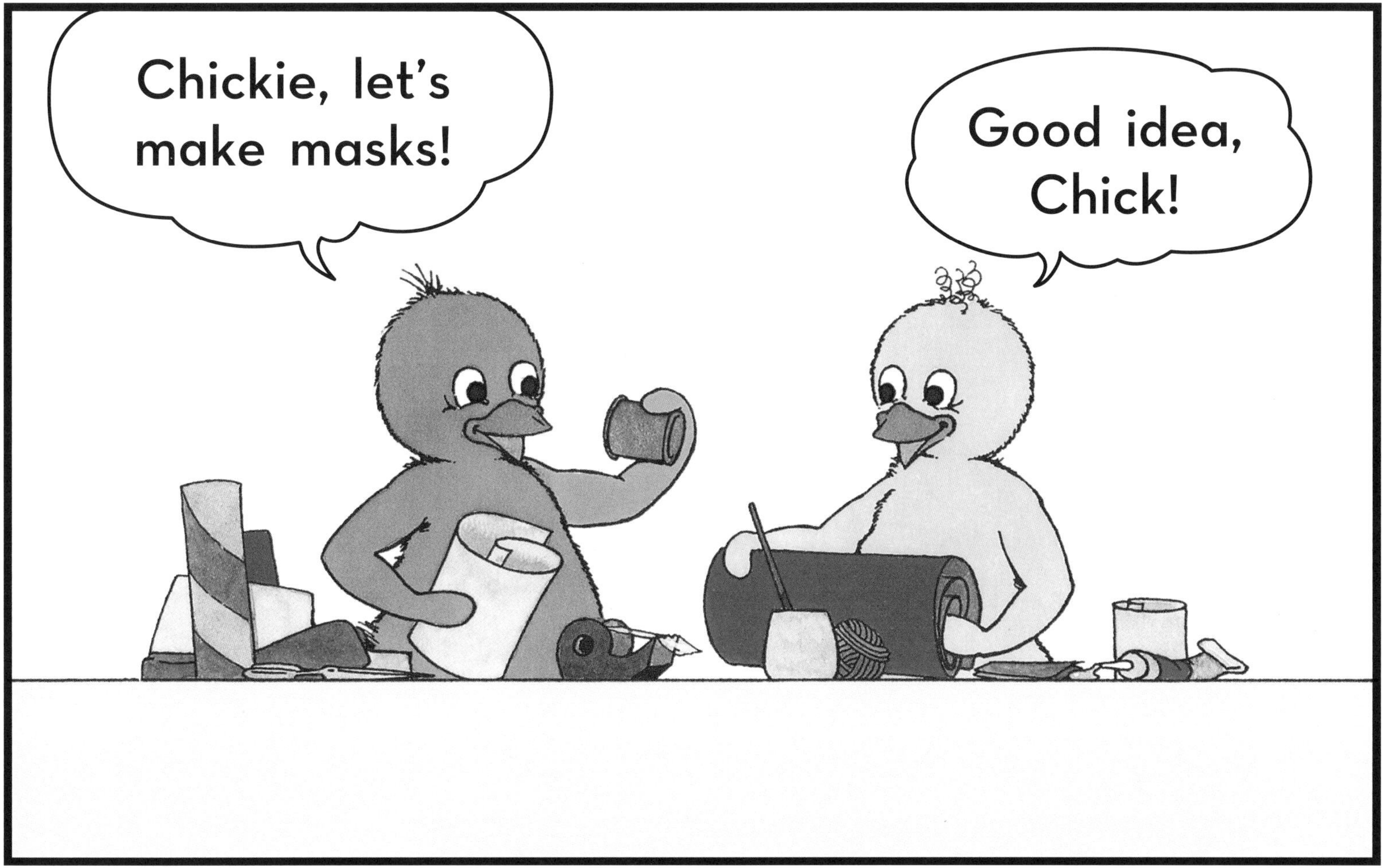
Chickie, let's make masks!
Good idea, Chick!

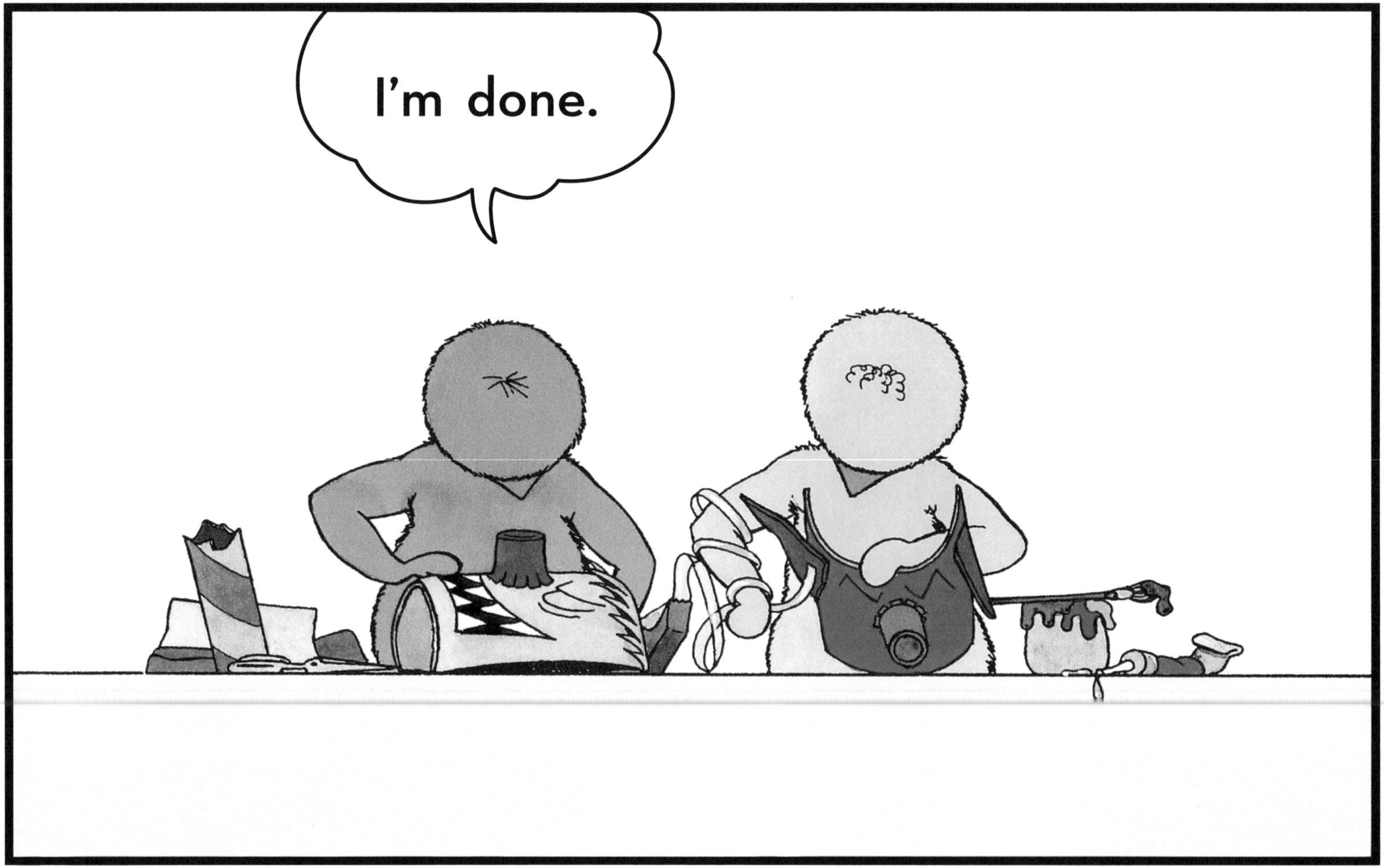
I'm done.

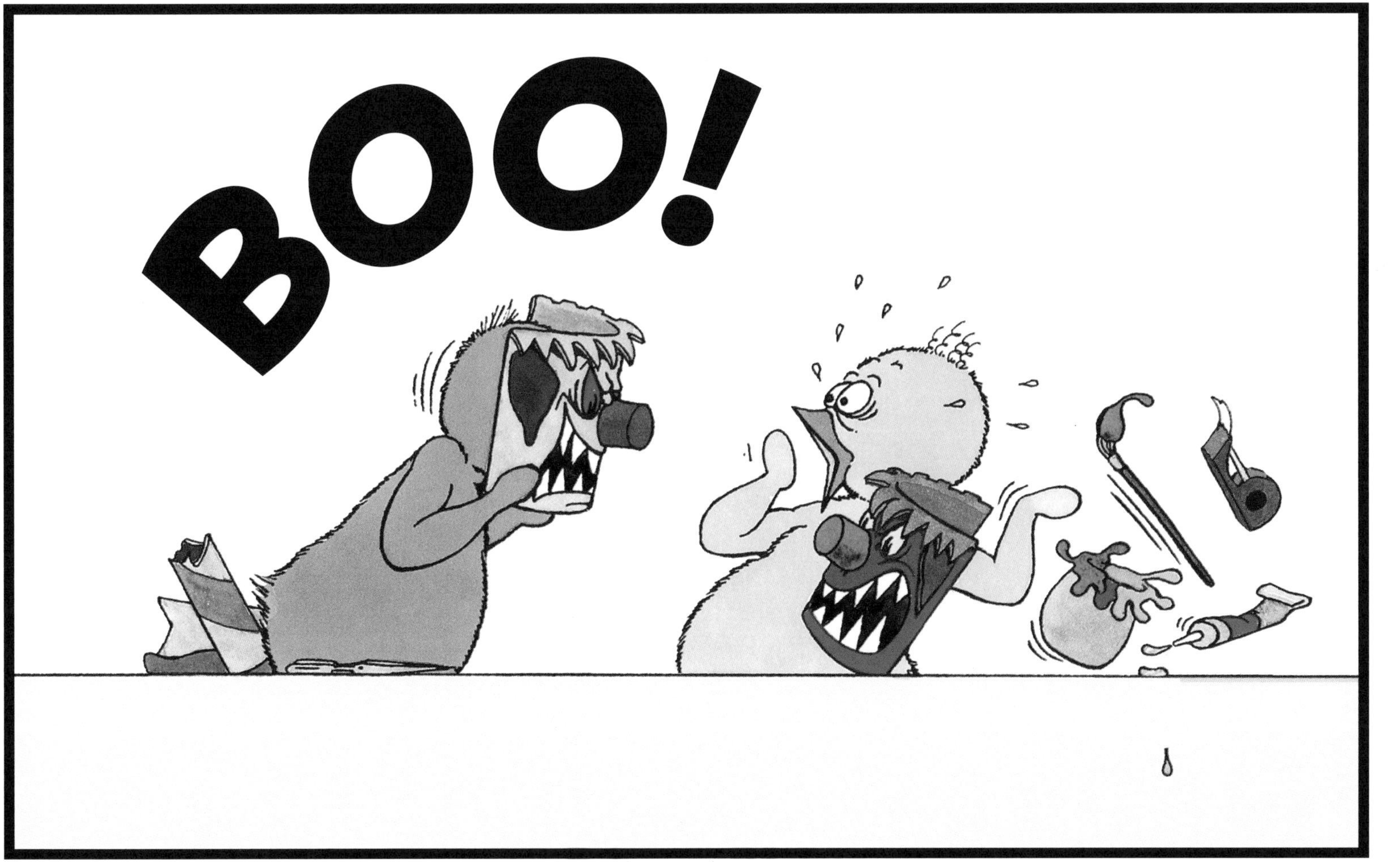
BOO!

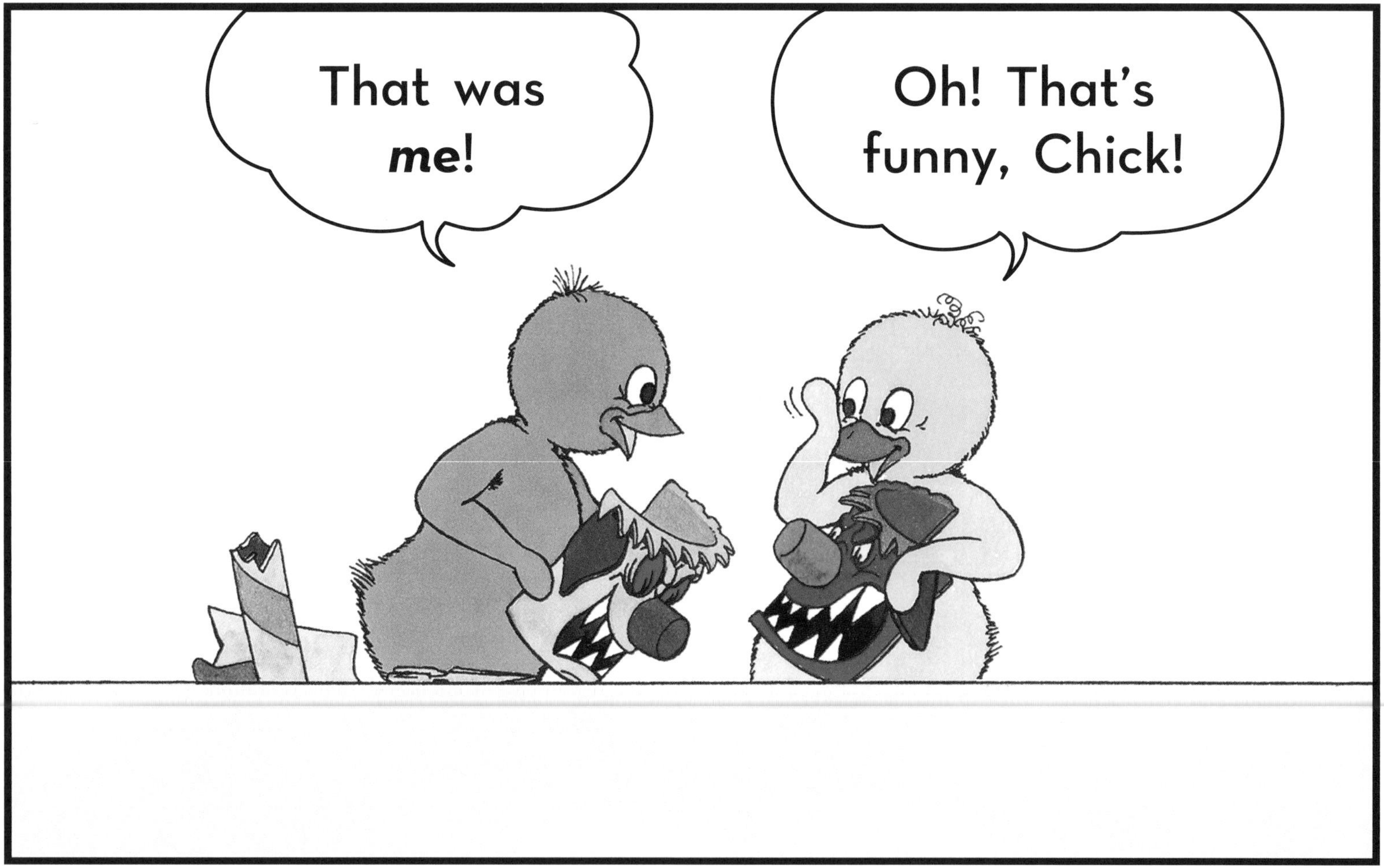
That was *me*!
Oh! That's funny, Chick!

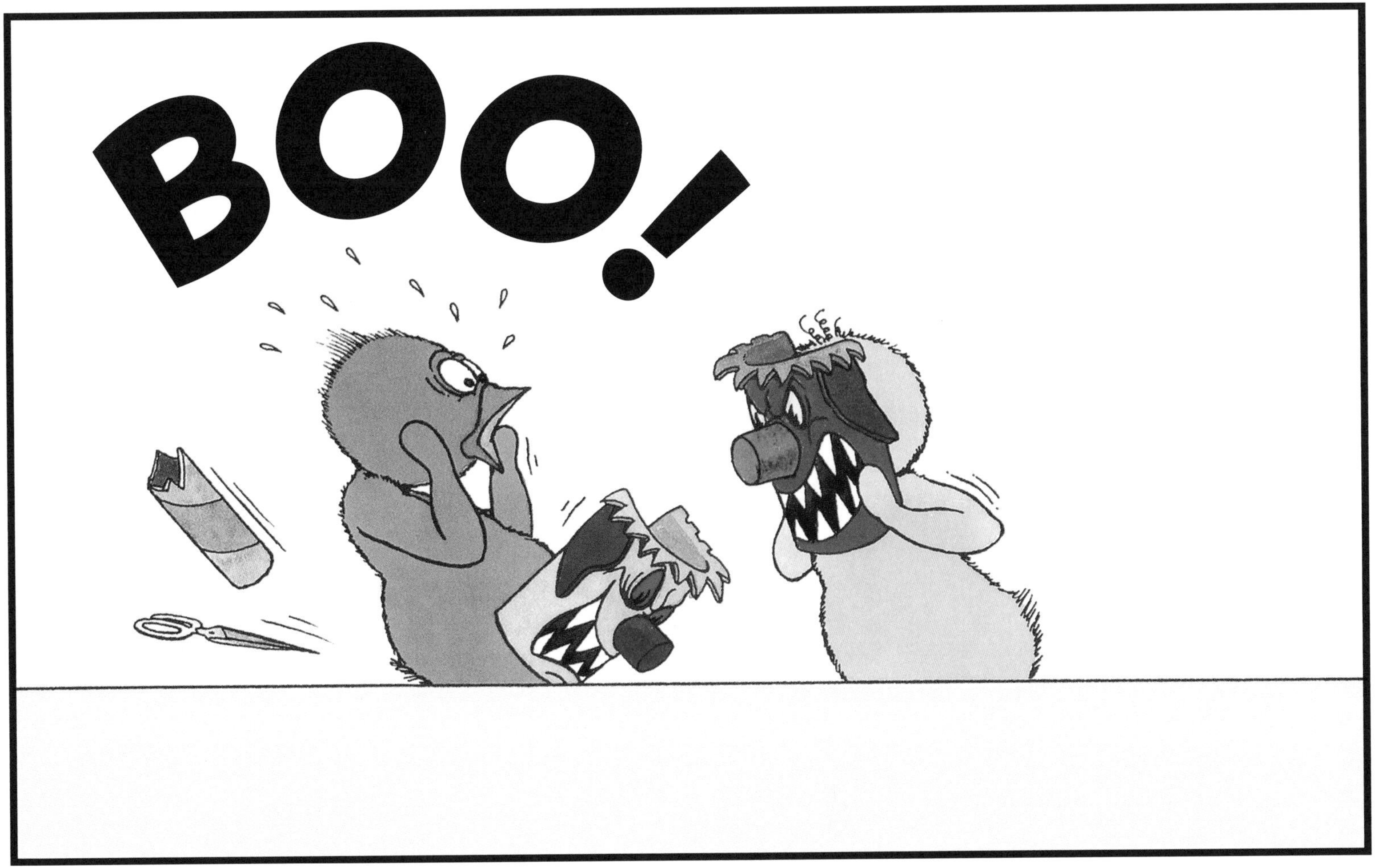
BOO!

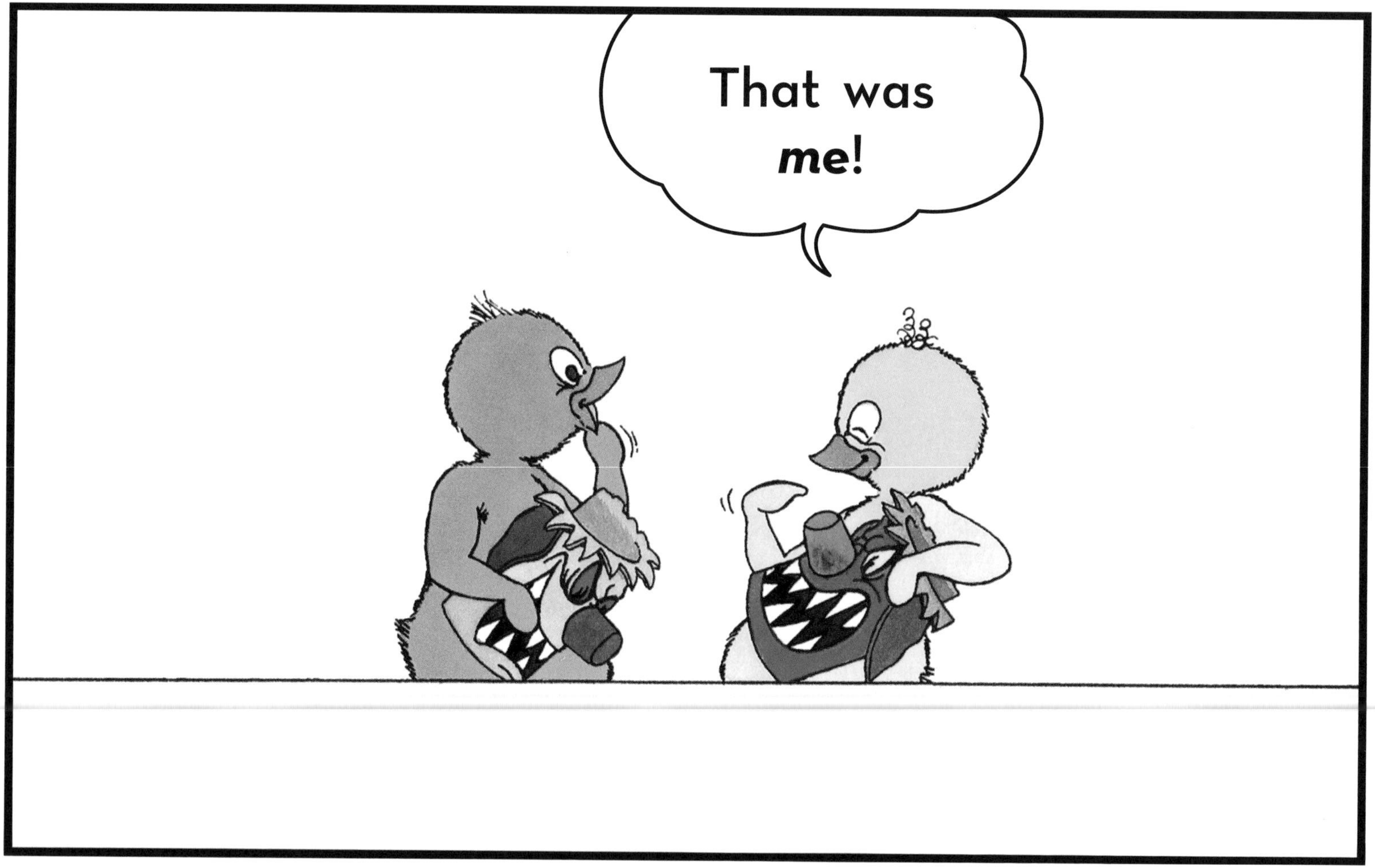
That was ***me***!

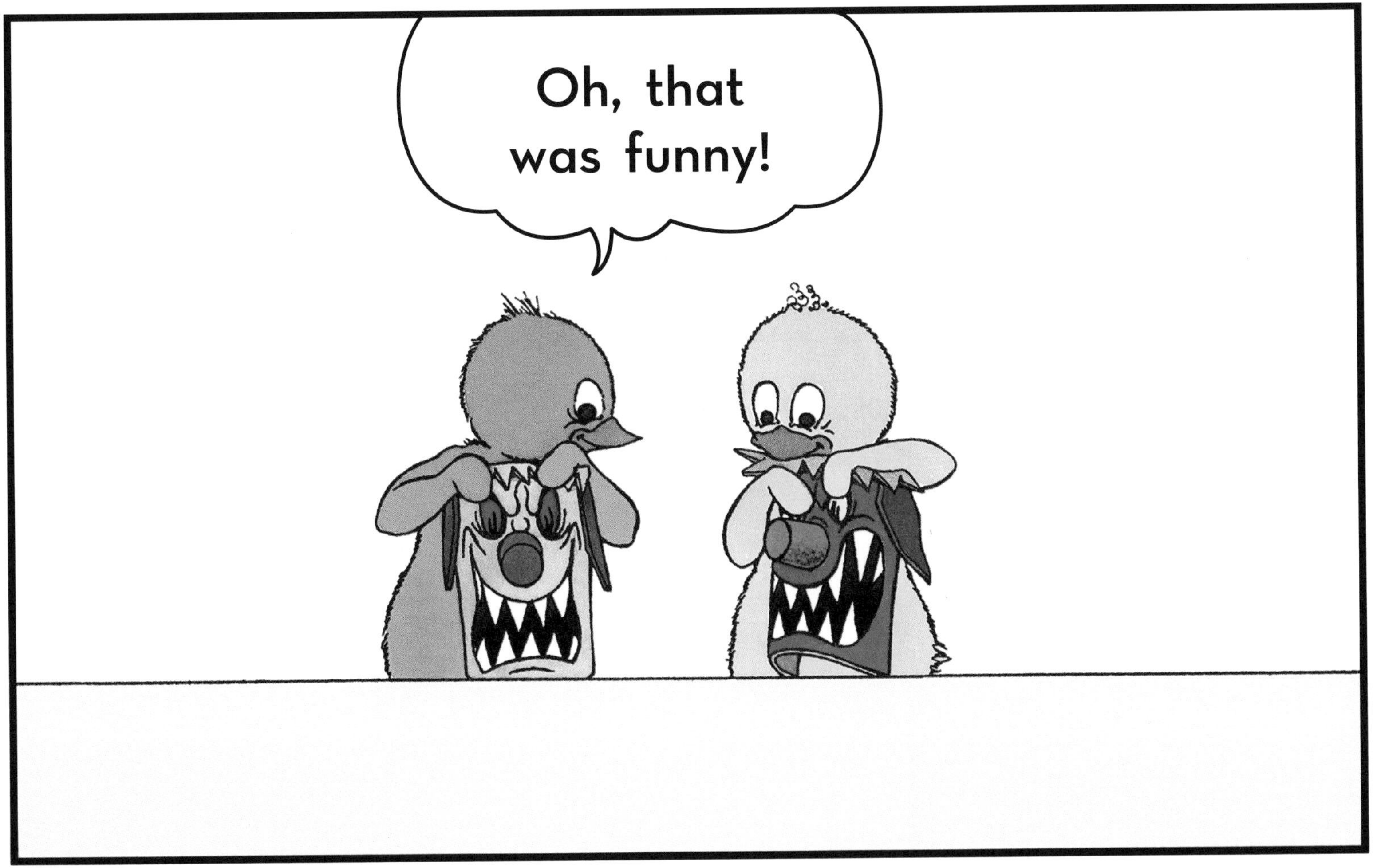
Oh, that was funny!

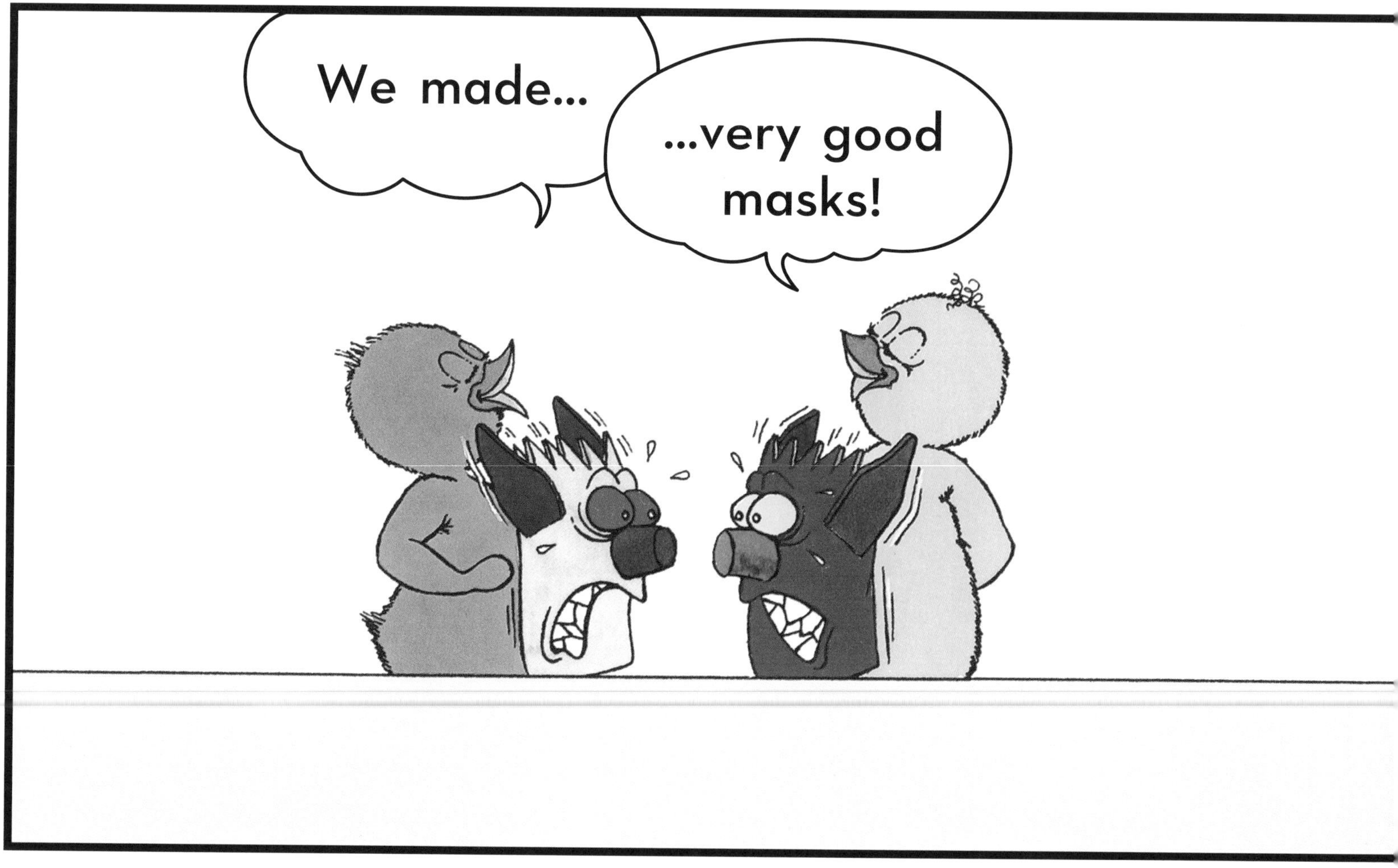
We made...
...very good masks!

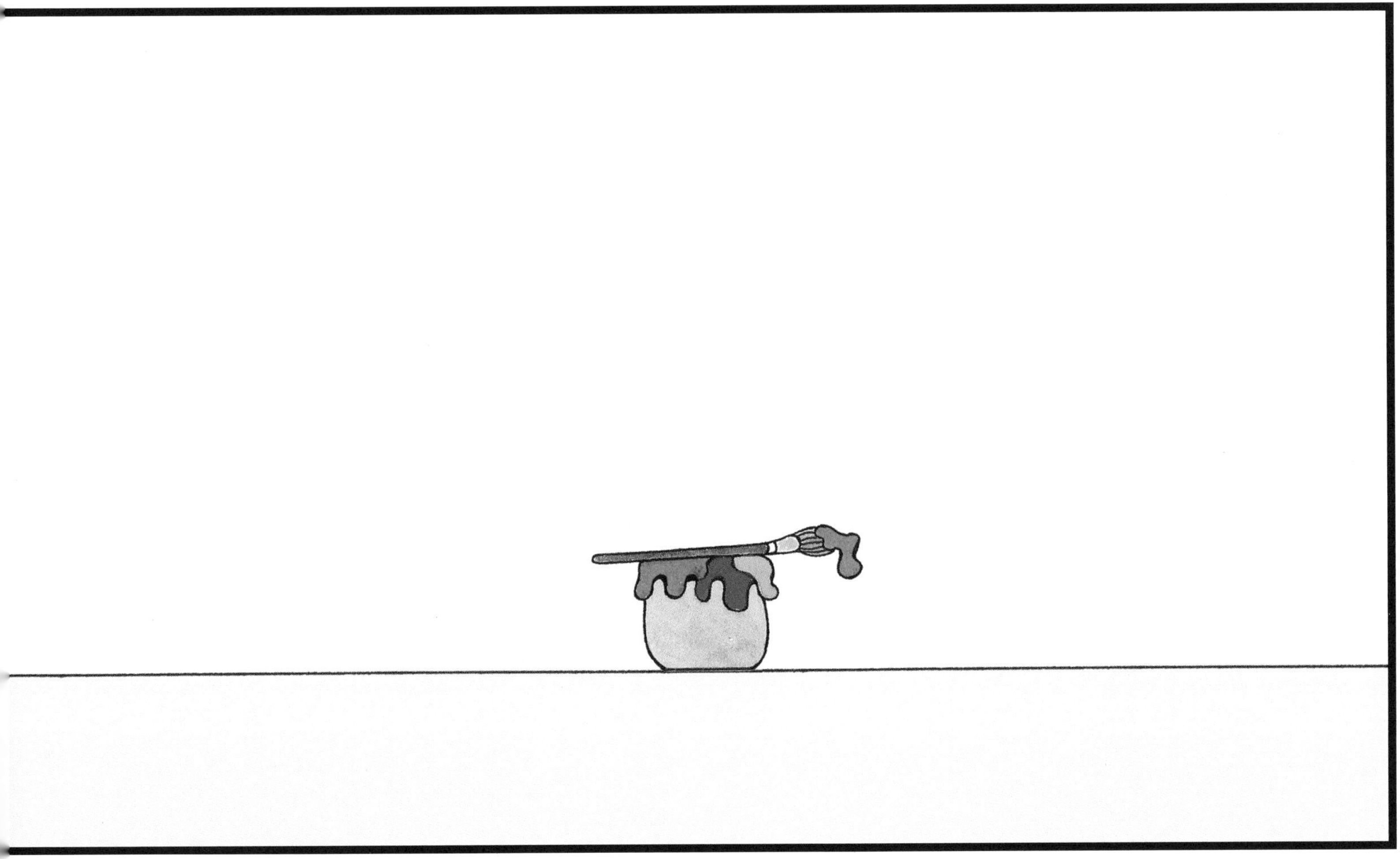

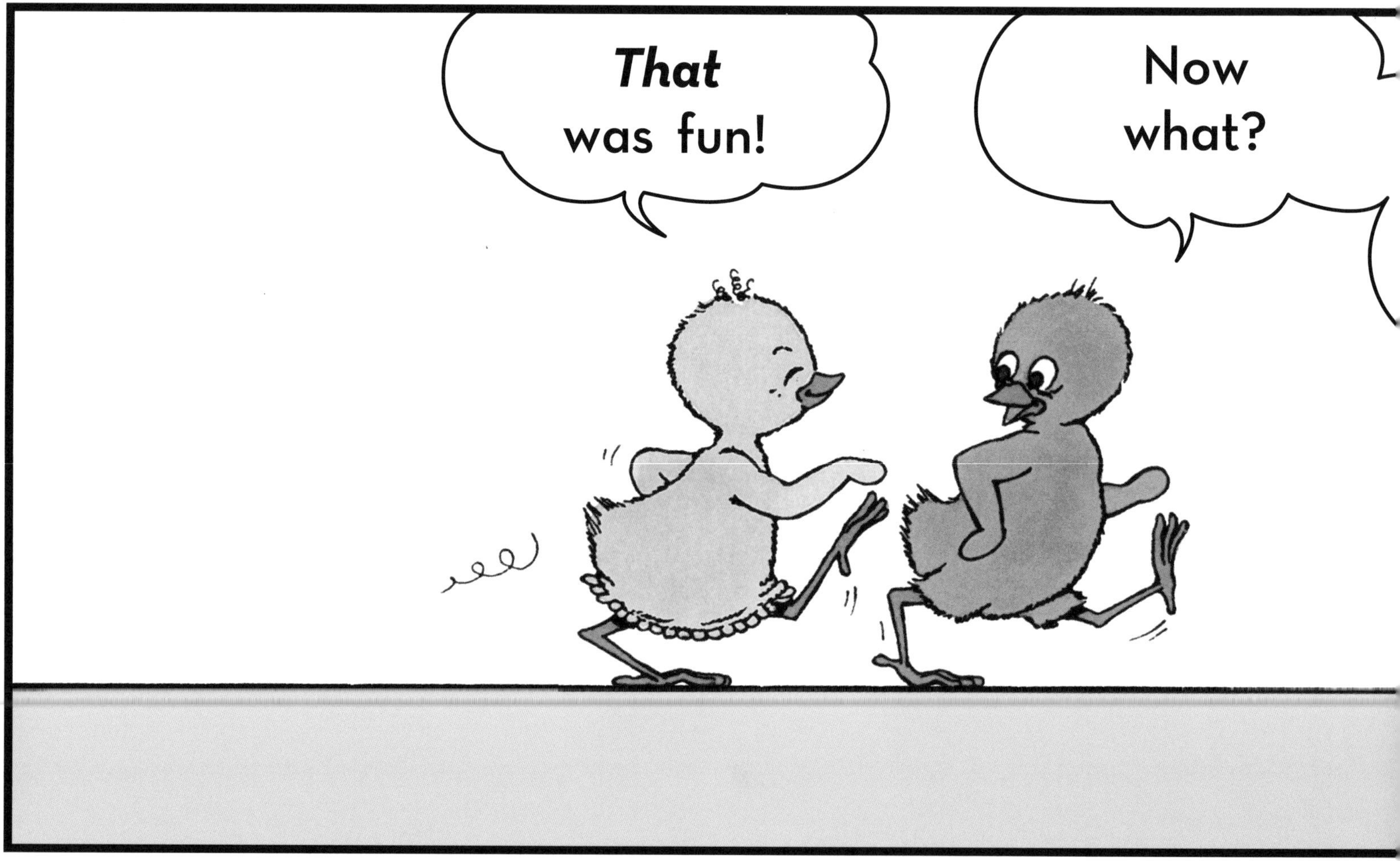
That was fun!
Now what?

What do *you* want to do?

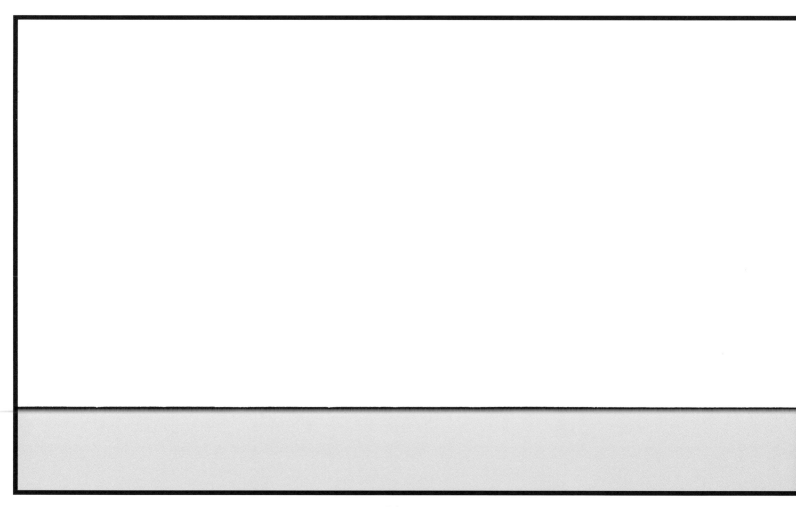

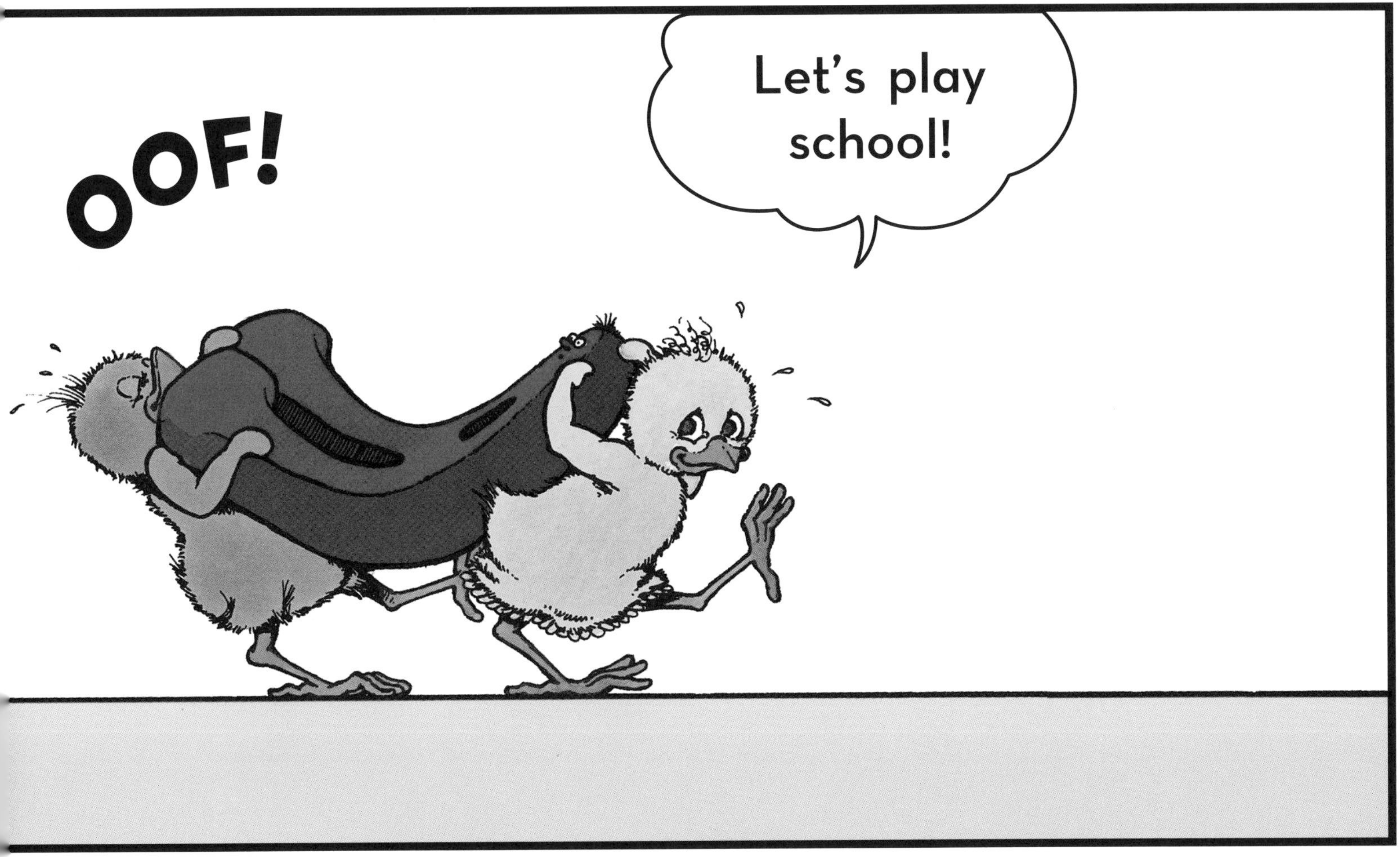
OOF!
Let's play school!

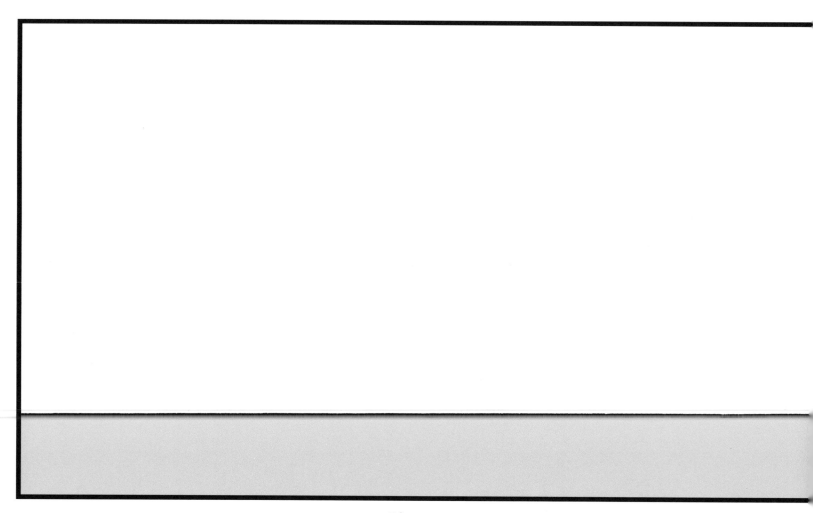

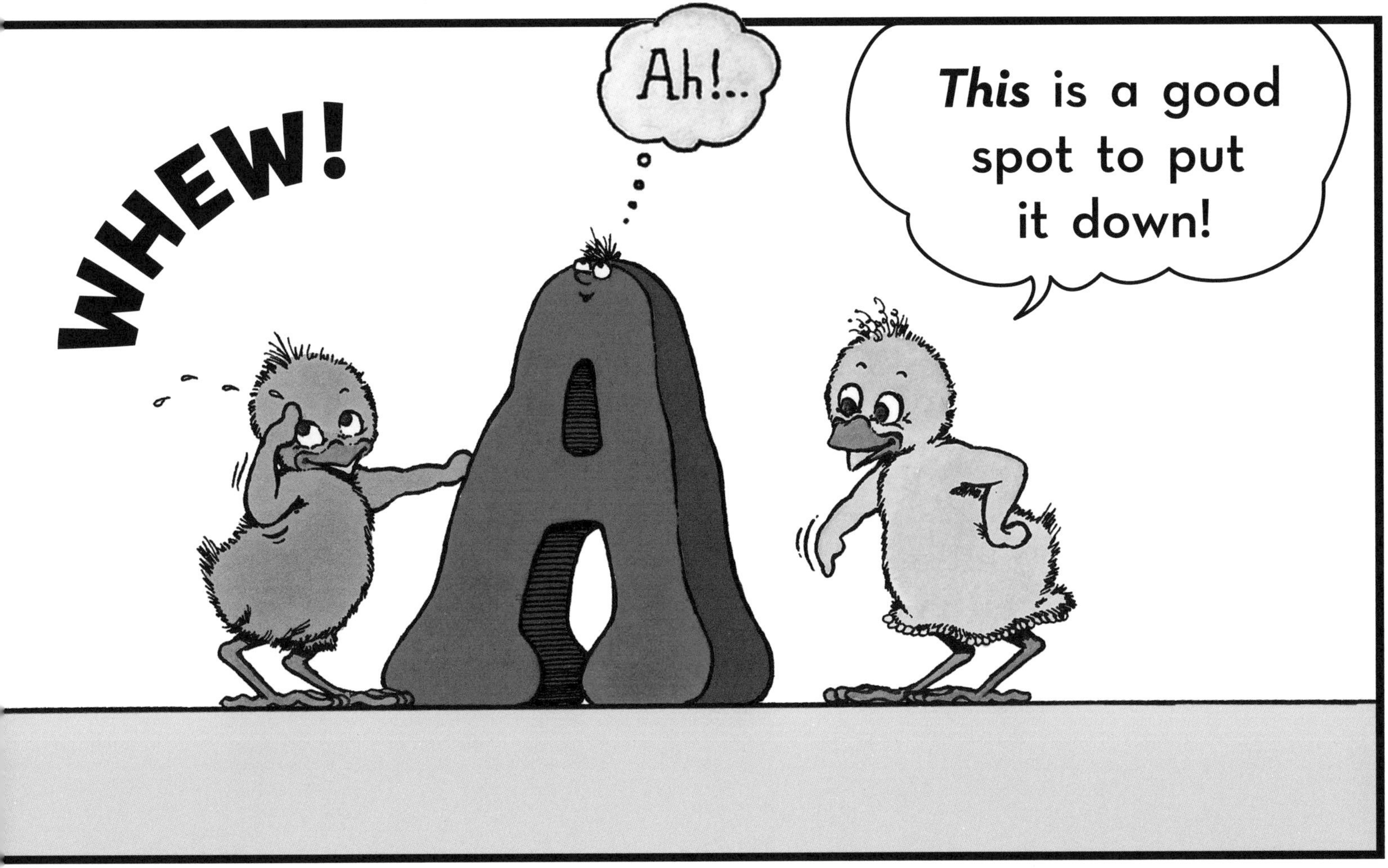
WHEW!
Ah!..
This is a good spot to put it down!

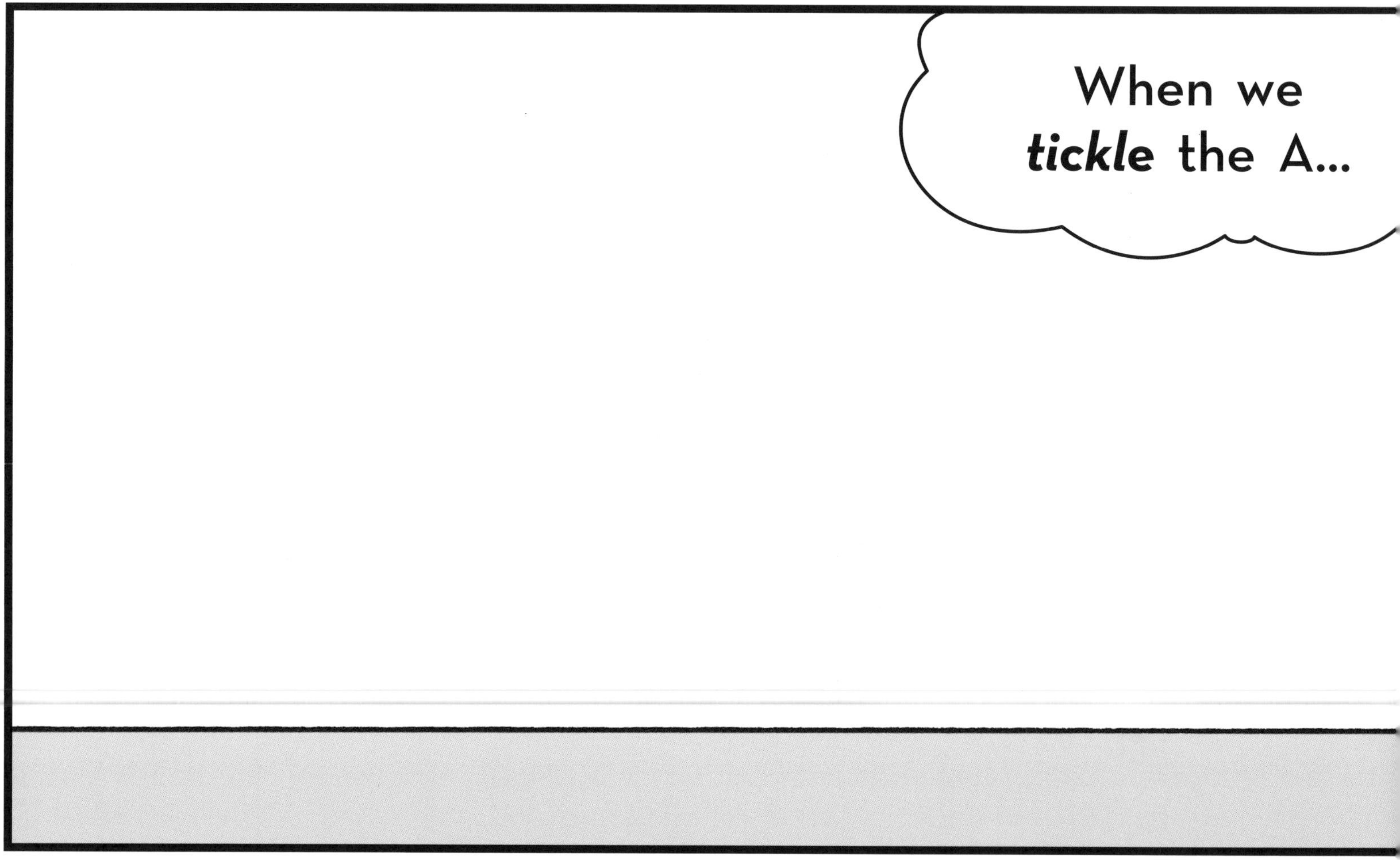
When we *tickle* the A...

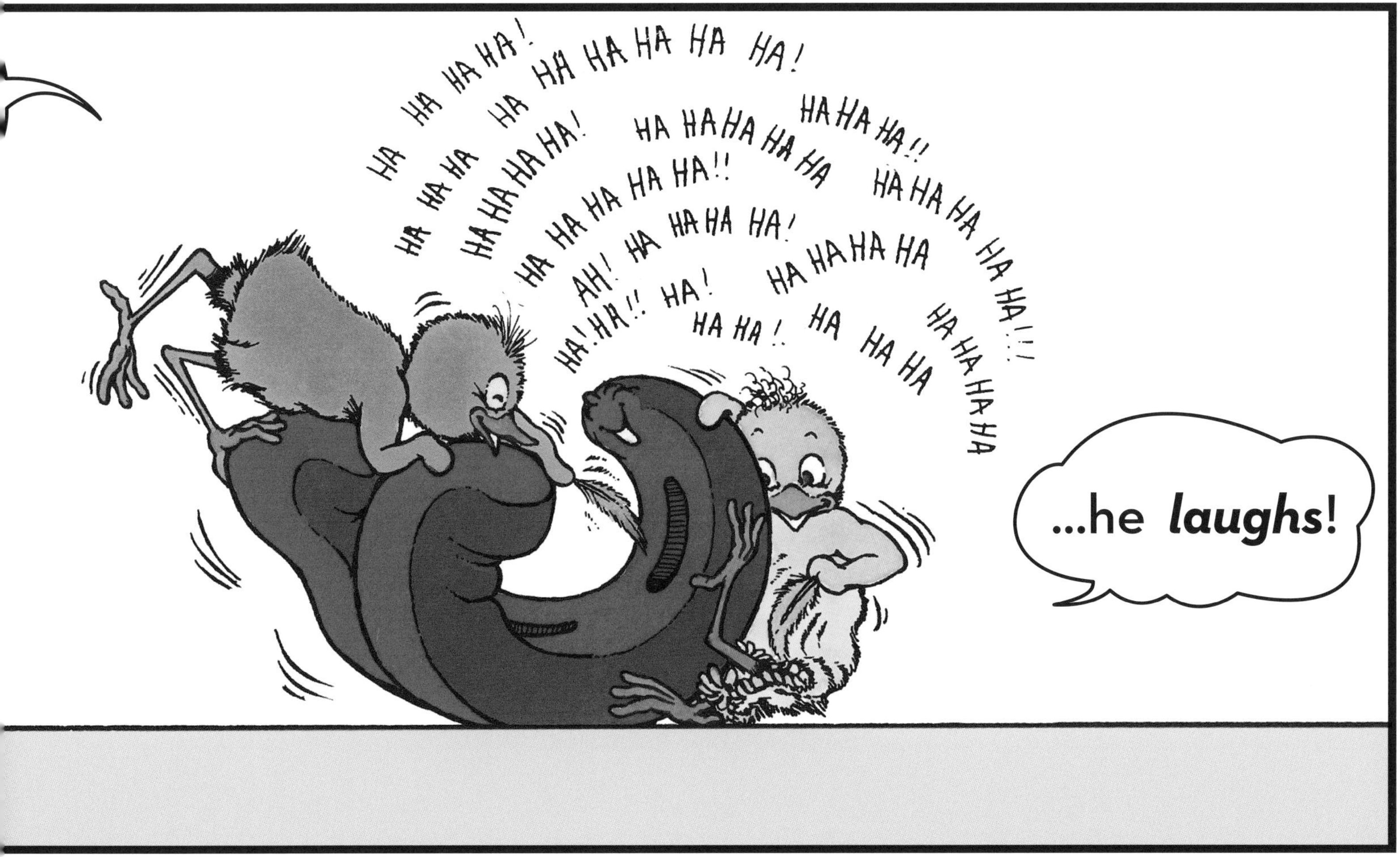
HA HA HA HA!
HA HA HA HA HA HA!
HA HA HA HA HA HA HA!
HA HA HA HA HA HA HA HA!!
HA HA HA HA HA HA
HA HA HA HA!!
AH! HA HA HA HA!
HA! HA!! HA!
HA HA!
HA HA HA HA
HA HA HA HA HA HA HA!!!
HA HA HA
HA HA HA HA HA
...he *laughs*!

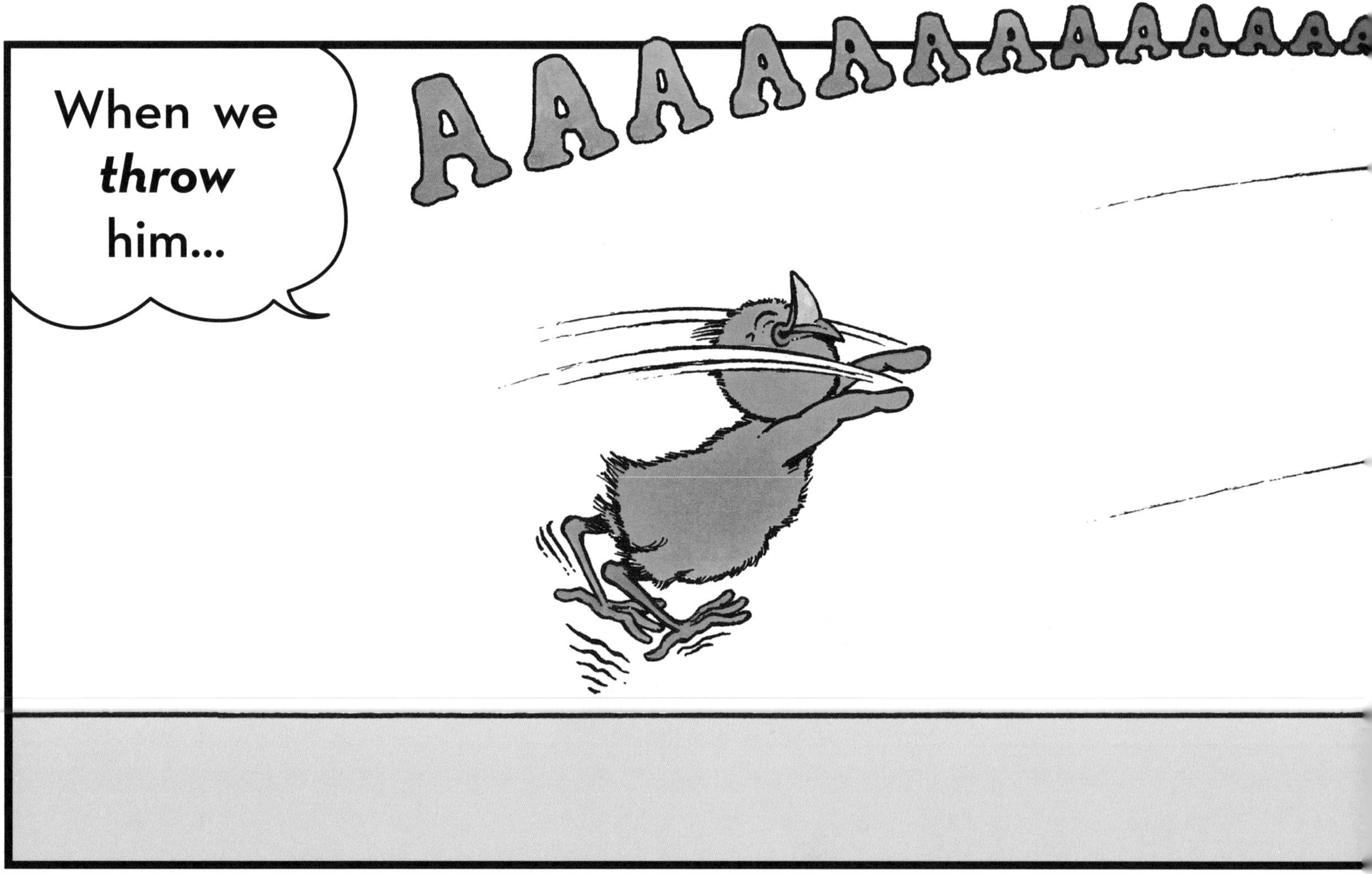
When we *throw* him...
AAAAAAAAAAAAA

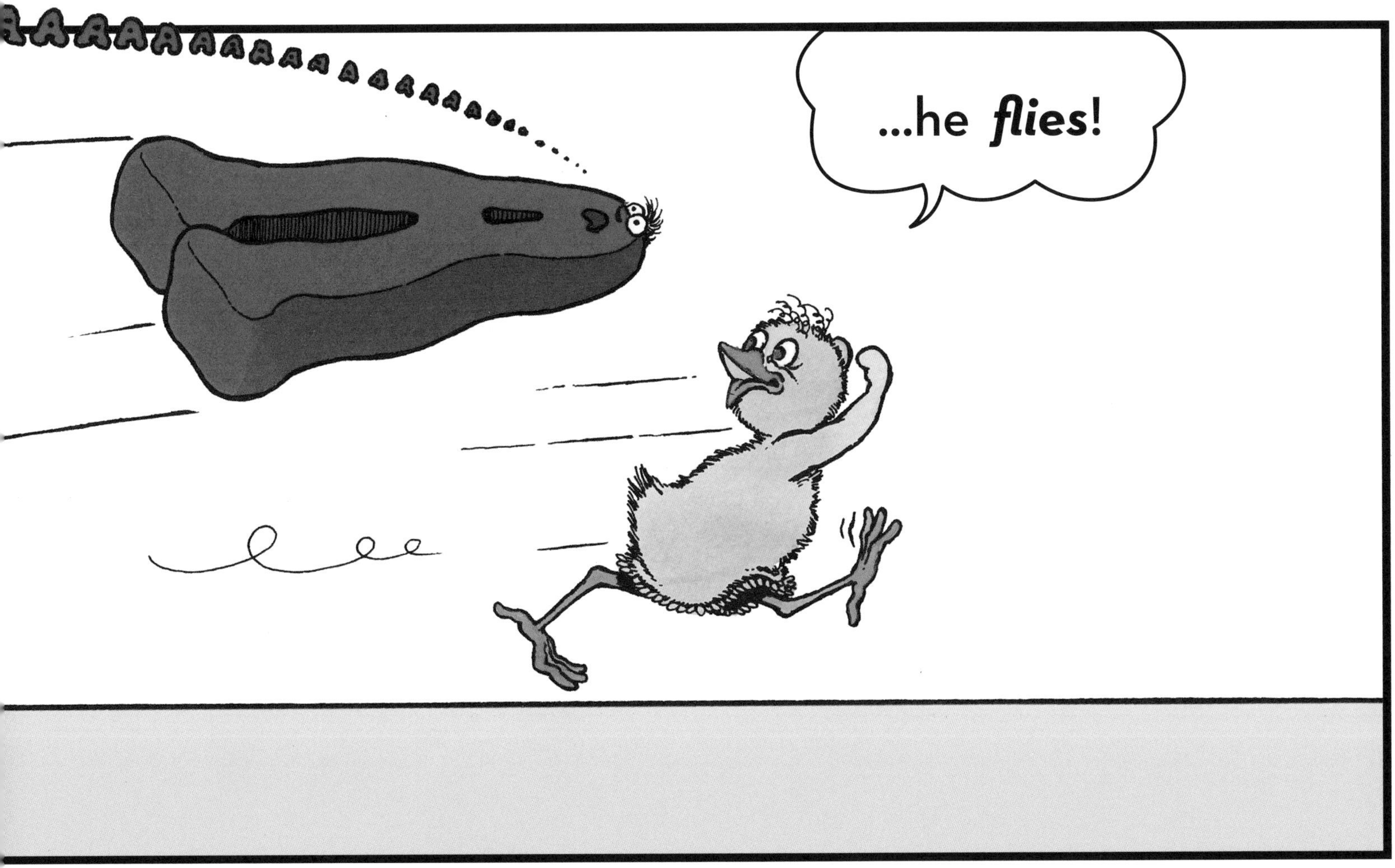

...he *flies*!

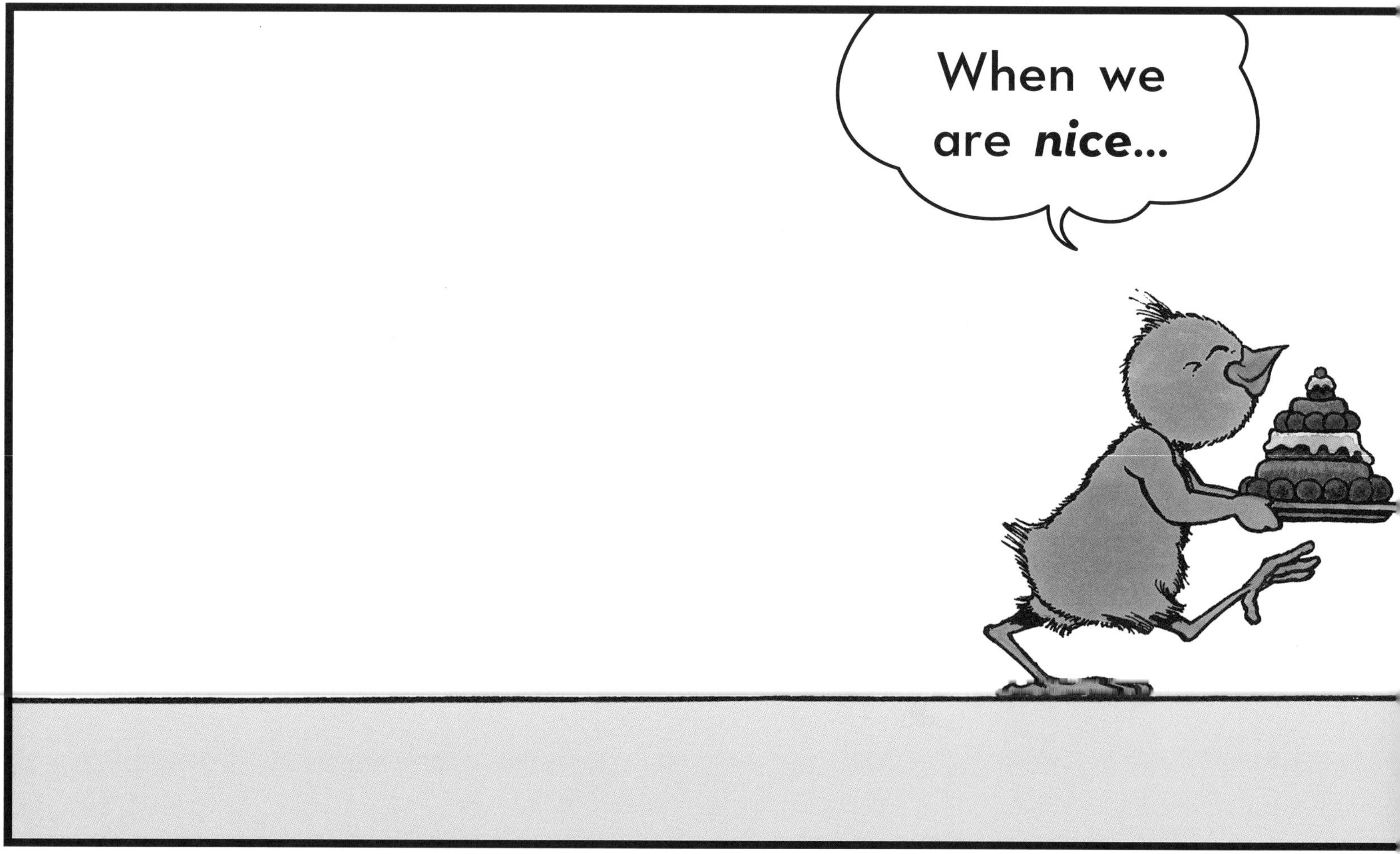
When we are ***nice***...

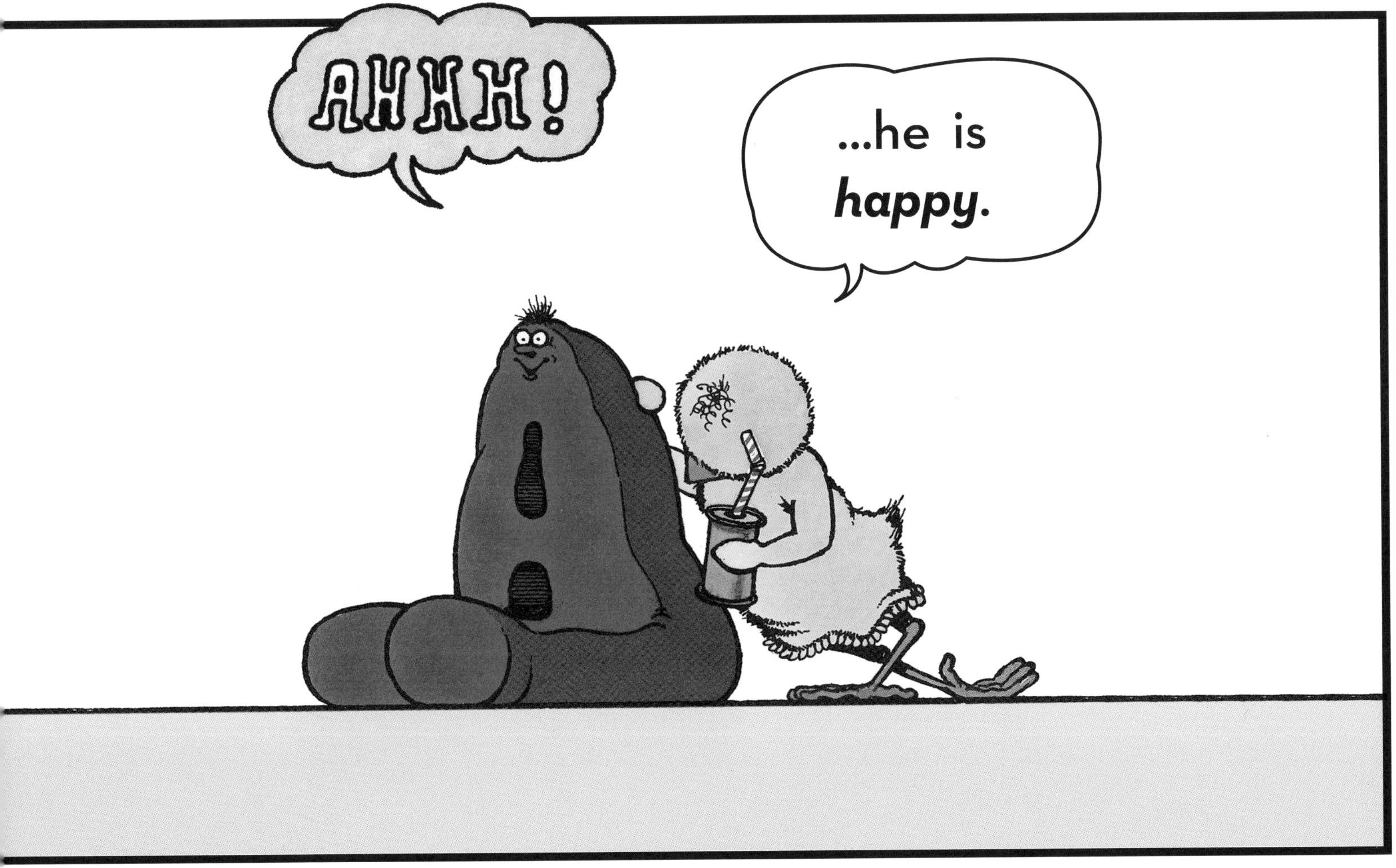
AHHH!
...he is *happy*.

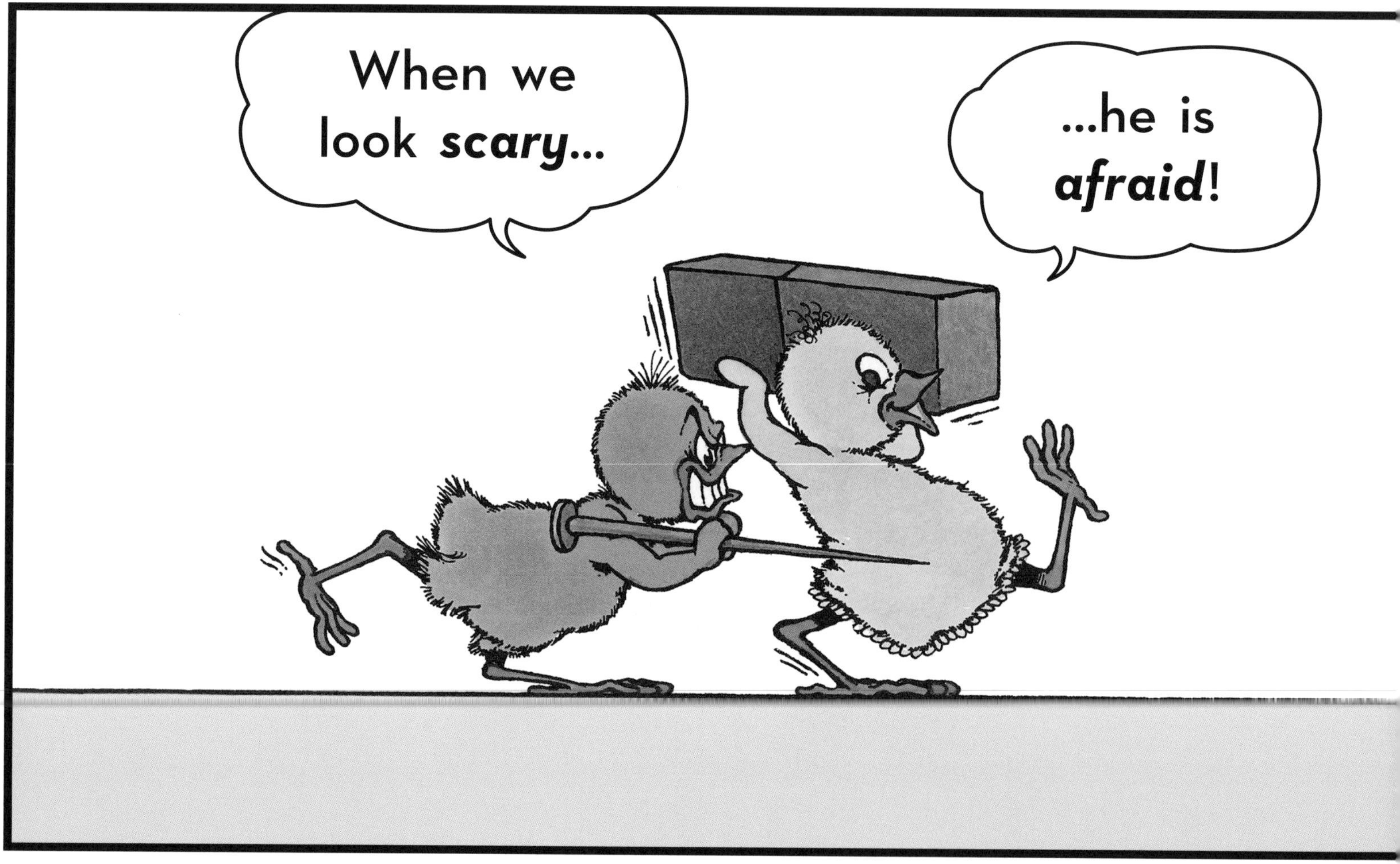
When we look ***scary***...
...he is ***afraid***!

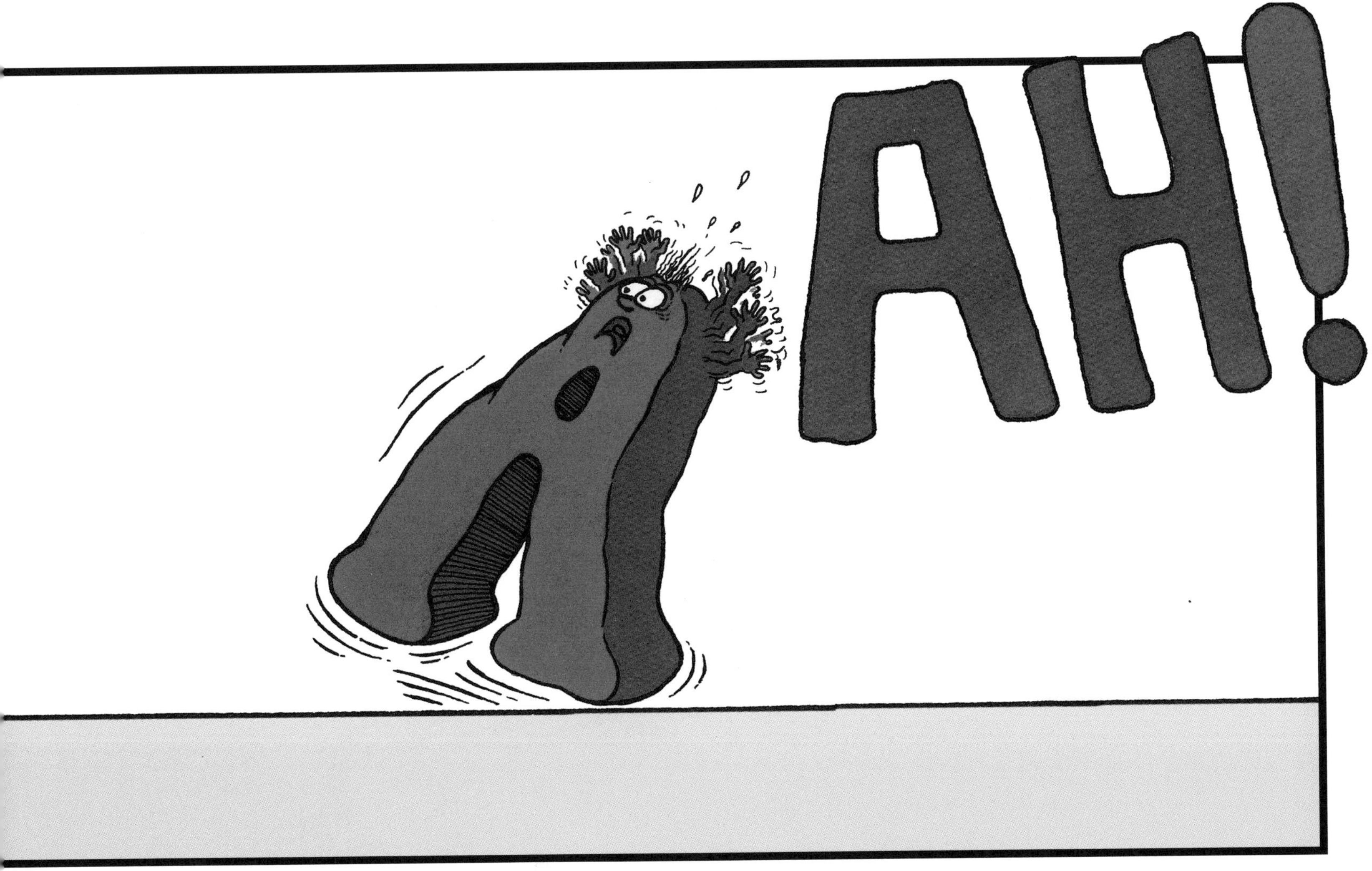
AH!

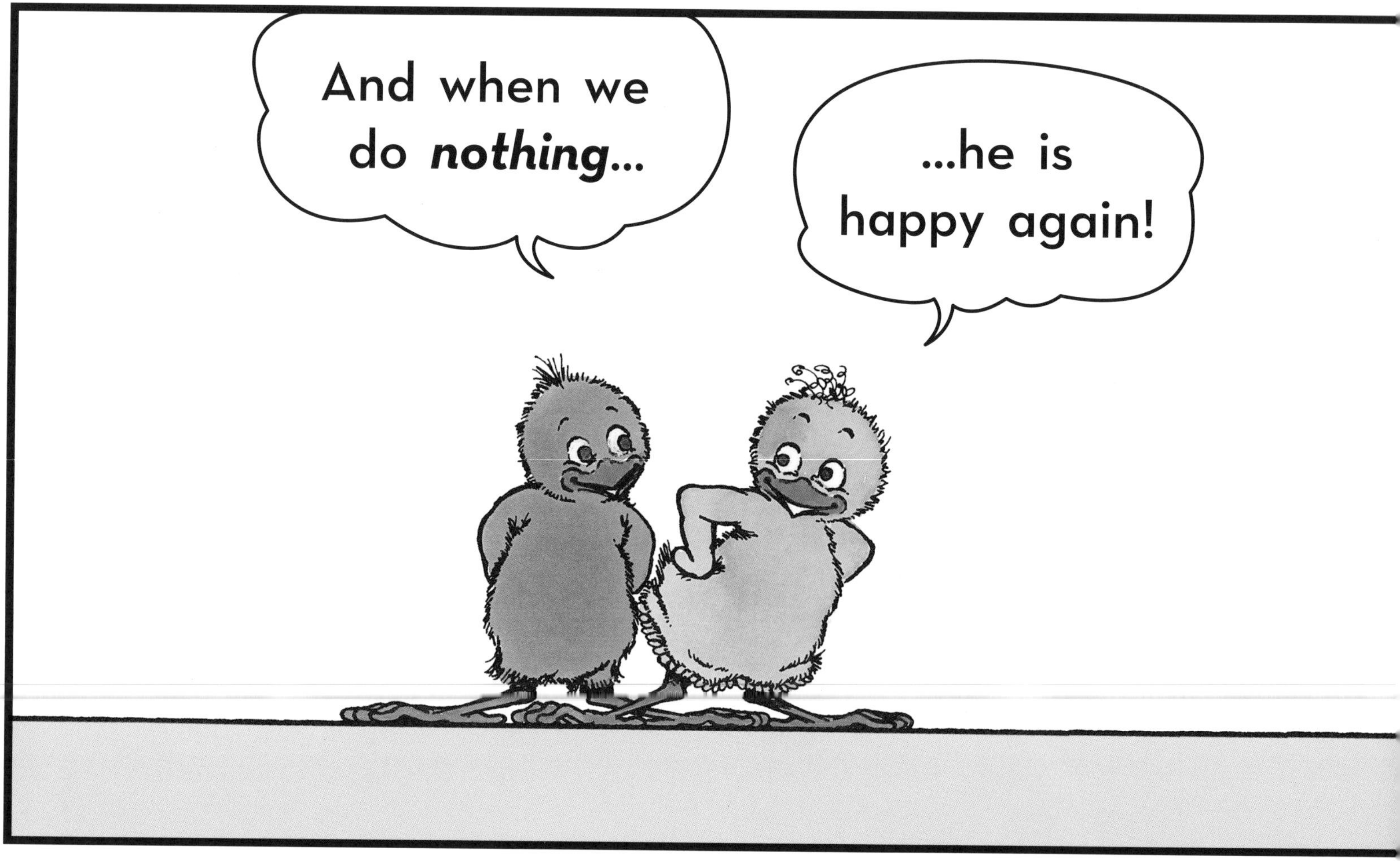
And when we do nothing...
...he is happy again!

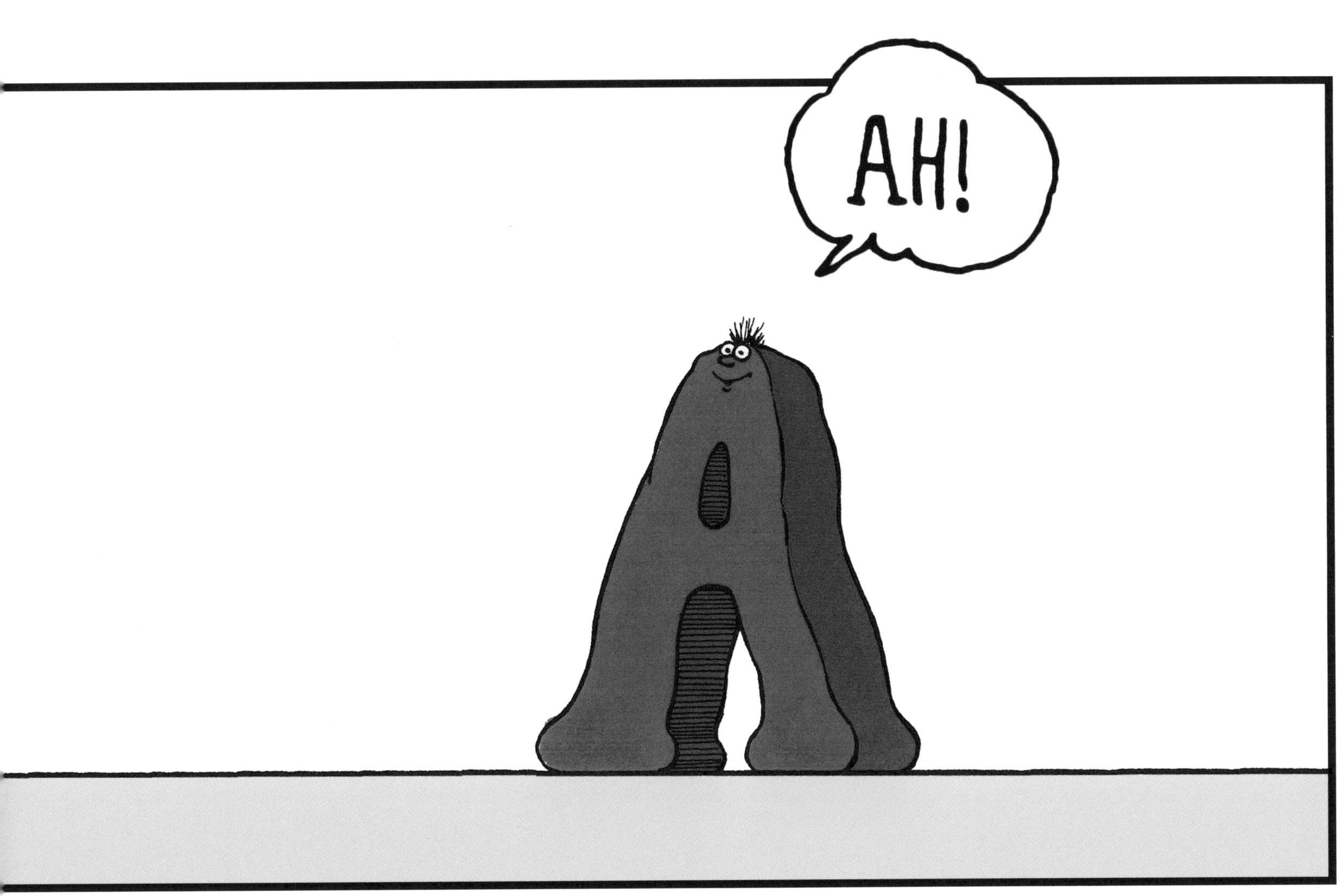
AH!

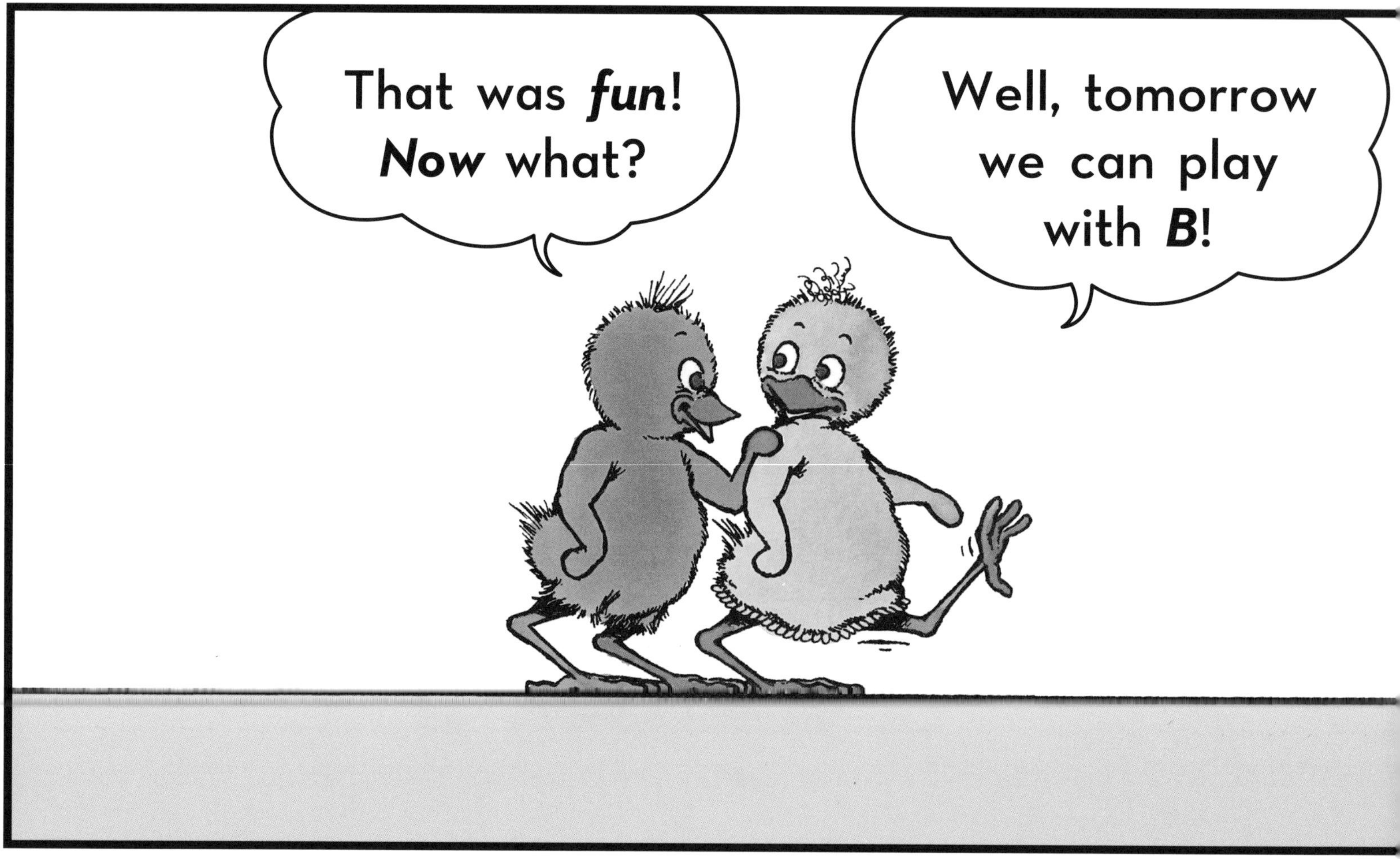
That was ***fun***! ***Now*** what?
Well, tomorrow we can play with ***B***!

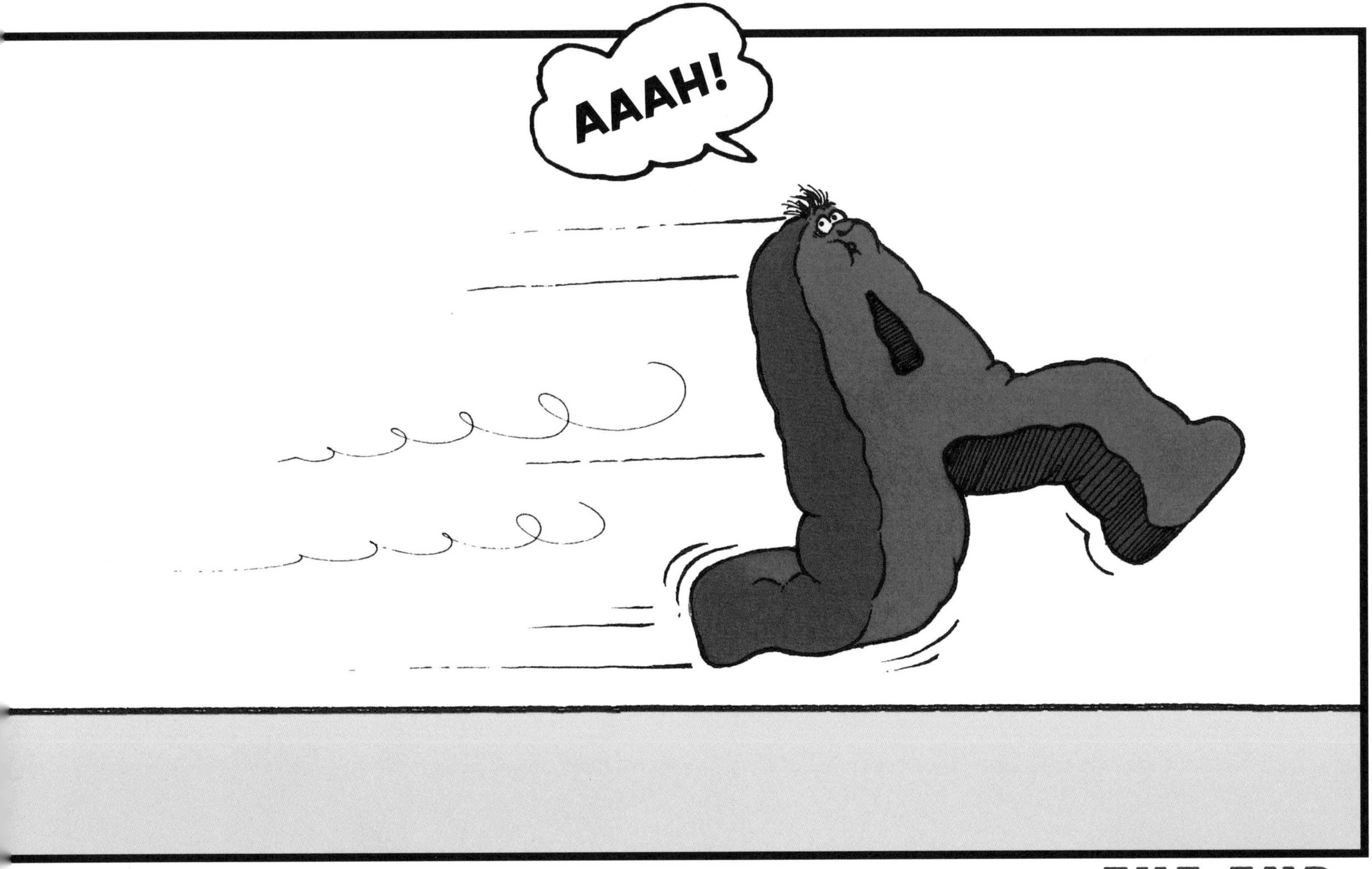
AAAH!

THE END

ABOUT THE AUTHOR

CLAUDE PONTI is a prolific author, painter and illustrator, beloved the world over for his humorous explorations of the nonsense world of dreams. The artist created his first picture book, *Adèle's Album,* to amuse his young daughter; he has since authored more than sixty children's books. On a personal note, Claude says: "I'm left-handed; I prefer cats to dogs (they don't lick people); and I'm not a vegetarian because I can't stand the cry of the lettuce or the carrot wrenched from the earth." He also fondly remembers climbing trees as a young boy, looking for the best spot to sit and read a book. He currently divides his time between the French countryside (where there are many birds, such as pheasants) and Paris (where there are pigeons).

TIPS FOR PARENTS AND TEACHERS:

HOW TO READ COMICS WITH KIDS

Kids love comics! They are naturally drawn to the details in the pictures, which make them want to read the words. Comics beg for repeated readings and let both emerging and reluctant readers enjoy complex stories with a rich vocabulary. But since comics have their own grammar, here are a few tips for reading them with kids:

GUIDE YOUNG READERS: Use your finger to show your place in the text, but keep it at the bottom of the speaking character so it doesn't hide the very important facial expressions.

HAM IT UP! Think of the comic book story as a play and don't hesitate to read with expression and intonation. Assign parts or get kids to supply the sound effects, a great way to reinforce phonics skills.

LET THEM GUESS. Comics provide lots of context for the words, so emerging readers can make informed guesses. Like jigsaw puzzles, comics ask readers to make connections, so check a young audience's understanding by asking "What's this character thinking?" (but don't be surprised if a kid finds some of the comics' subtle details faster than you).

TALK ABOUT THE PICTURES. Point out how the artist paces the story with pauses (silent panels) or speeded-up action (a burst of short panels). Discuss how the size and shape of the panels carry meaning.

ABOVE ALL, ENJOY! There is of course never one right way to read, so go for the shared pleasure. Once children make the story happen in their imagination, they have discovered the thrill of reading, and you won't be able to stop them. At that point, just go get them more books, and more comics.

www.TOON-BOOKS.com

SEE OUR FREE ONLINE CARTOON MAKERS, LESSON PLANS, AND MUCH MORE